The Boatyard Murder

and

other short stories

Author's Note

All characters portrayed are creatures
of the author's imagination
and bear no relationship to any living person.
Residences, companies and situations
are non-existent

ABA

First published in England
01.11.02
By Alex Brown Associates (Publishers)
Cranes Lane Lathom Nr Ormskirk L40 5UJ
Lancashire UK
Tel/ Fax 01695 572581
e-mail Ealexbrown@AOL.com
ISBN 0-9542335-1-4
All Rights Reserved
Copyright
ABA Publishers
Printed in England

The Boatyard Murder

And

other short stories

Alex Brown

ABA
Publishers

4

Contents

The Christmas Message
The Boatyard Murder
Vin L'mour
The Trip
The Angel of Mercy
Jacques Le Merc

Introduction

In preparing the introduction to this first series of short stories I am reminded of another writer who approached the subject with the same intrepidation as I...
" I have come legally to man's estate...I make a respectable income by...reporting the debates in Parliament for a Morning Newspaper. Night after night I record predictions that never come to pass, professions that are never fulfilled...I have come out in another way. I have taken with fear and trembling to authorship, I write a little something, in secret, and send it to a magazine...Since then, I have taken heart to write a good many trifling pieces."----------- Thus in *David Copperfield*, and through the mouth of its hero, Dickens tells of his first step to fame. The "little something" and other "trifling pieces" was first published in 1836 as Sketches by Boz

The Christmas Message

"You can always tell when Christmas is around the corner," said Dena Jones collecting the post from the doormat. "The mail goes haywire and the Christmas card stakes are about to get under way."

"I see Aunt Evelyn's first again with her Christmas card," said Vikki, her youngest daughter, recognising the immaculate script on the envelope.

8

There were five of us into this Christmas card game. Mom was the pillar on which we all leaned. A young looking forty-two year old, ex-computer programmer at the local glass works, she still retained her good looks. Then there was Dad, the rock on which the pillar was built. Frank, at fourteen, was the eldest of the kids; he was the quiet one. Then there was Julie and me, the youngest, all anxious to see if anything interesting had come through the letterbox.

It was five days before Christmas. Being first downstairs, I had collected the mail on my way to the kitchen, where breakfast was laid, and started to sift through the letters, when suddenly my eyes came across a stranger in the pack. It was a Christmas card of course, but different. The envelope was long and thin with a foreign stamp and strange overprinting. Turning it over I looked at the seal wondering if I might just…

"Good morning Vikki. Is that the mail?" Mom stomped in collecting the envelopes from my hands as she walked by. It was rude I thought, but maybe there was a reason. I know Saturdays are busy for her with us all around her neck most of the day. Dad was last down but we all waited for him to join us for breakfast. It was just a Saturday routine we'd got used to.

During the meal we each took our mail but the special envelope had gone. I remember plainly that there were six but now there were only five. I looked around the table but the special one was nowhere to be seen.

My thoughts were full of the envelope all day. Then, later, following her weekly session at the gym I noted Mom's handbag on the sideboard. I shouldn't have done it I know, but I just couldn't resist a peep.

"Vikki," Mom called from the kitchen. I could hear her approaching footsteps on the tiled floor "Vikki, hang your coat up, dear. You know I don't like clothes strewn about the furniture."

My heart was going ten to the dozen. "Sorry, Mom, I forgot," I said, managing to distance myself from the handbag. But it was there; I had seen it slotted into one of the sections.

The maintenance of high voltage electrical distribution cables is John Jones's job in life. He climbs the pylons that carry the electricity over the face of the earth. It is a dangerous job, working next to thousands of volts high above the ground, and safety standards are being continually monitored and improved.

John is two years older than his wife, Dena, and the grey streaks starting to tint his black, well-groomed hair, only add to his distinguished looks. At his peak of fitness he walks with a comfortable upright gait.

It had been late in October when John with a number of other employees had been invited by their company to attend a weekend course in Paris on Safety Methods. Wives and partners had been included.

They had booked into their hotel near to the Paris Opera and the arrangements were for the men to meet for their course of instruction on Saturday at 10 am. The ladies would be collected an hour later, outside the Opera for a tour of the city.

"Have a nice day love, I wish I was joining you," said John, taking his wife in his arms. "I've got a boring day of Safety Methods."

Breaking free, Dena stared into her husband's eyes. "Now look here, John Jones, I have come all this way because I hate your rotten job, and because I love you. I live in fear and dread of you having an accident working up there in the sky. I want you to go to these meetings with positive thoughts. It's your life they are respecting."

"Yes, I am sure you are right, love," he responded. "Anyway, let's both have a good day and tonight we'll make up for it," he concluded with a broad grin.

She could see the difference in her mother since that card had arrived. She'd peeped into the purse again but the envelope had gone. It was nowhere to be found and she knew in her heart that it hadn't been destroyed.

Mom looked younger, she had changed her hairstyle and it suited her. Dad had bought her a new dress for Christmas and it was the new length, perfect to show off her lovely legs. She looked radiant and went about the house singing. It was irritating not knowing what was going on.

The Parisian taxi driver had been slow. He had preferred talking to driving, and she had missed the coach. But she wasn't disappointed; she could get by without coach trips in Paris. The Opera district had much to offer and she decided on a visit to the Musee de Louvre and, by way of a personal tip, she would call at a corner café for a coffee and cognac.

There were just a few managerial types in the corner and she took a seat in the window and looked out on the passing traffic.

"Madam, bonjour," said the waiter.

"Bonjour, Monsieur. Café and cognac si'l vous plais..."

The traffic was busy that morning and the men in the corner were having a heated discussion, when the door opened and a smartly dressed man entered, passing a greeting to her en route to his colleagues.

Her thoughts wandered to John at the conference, she prayed that he would always be kept safe in his job.

"Madam, excusez moi. Are you alone?"

She had a disgusting habit of blushing, she didn't know why, but she couldn't avoid it, and her make-up didn't hide it.

"Er-no, er – yes." It was him. He had left his colleagues to serve her coffee that had stood on the bar. God, he wasn't only good looking he had everything to match.

He sat beside her. "I don't wish to intrude, but I can see that you are not familiar with this area and a lady alone in Paris is not good."

They talked in broken French. He was polite in his approach, mannerly and not overstepping the mark in his comments. Everything about him was admirable. When she had finished her coffee she rose to leave, but stumbled; her legs had gone to water. He caught her in his arms, releasing her immediately. He then stepped outside to help her over the step.

"But you cannot go to the Louvre alone, Dena," he said. "Please let me show you my city, the parts that tourists never see,"

His French accent was soft and gentle like the songbirds in heaven, she thought.

"You see I have the rest of the day free and I would bring you back to your hotel in time for your husband's return, ne c'est pas."

This is crazy! How could she be considering his offer? She was a married woman with three grown up kids. But, what the hell, let's push out the boat!

"I will accept on condition that you promise to return me to this café for six pm precisely."

"I agree," he said, putting his hand on his heart. "I promise."

His car was parked at the nearby insurance offices where he worked. The roof was down. She placed a scarf over her hair and she could feel the refreshing breeze skimming the top of her head. She had walked down this boulevard many times, but never, never been driven like this.

He was smiling at her and she smiled back. He placed his hand on hers and her heart missed a beat. She had no idea where they were going, she just didn't care, she had left all reality behind. She recalled a friend saying that the good lookers are all right at a distance, but when you get close up there is always a catch. But catch or no, she was his; she was his just for the asking.

They went to the shops were the elite Parisian ladies shopped, not in the thoroughfares, but in discreet passages which opened out to magnificent displays of luxurious items. Michel bought her a small phial of perfume. Of course she would never use it. They lunched at the George Cinq and then disappeared into the wonders of private Paris. She met his personal friends at a private club and sailed on the lake at the Bois de Bologne

It had been seven hours of heaven and now they were back at the café. They had talked of love, Michel was divorced and she had talked of John. They kept nothing secret.

"Well, my darling," he murmured, taking her into his arms, "and now we must part." She closed her eyes to remember this moment and he kissed her. They paused for that final second and with a last embrace he was gone.

She could tell the card was from him and her prying daughter must not set eyes on it, or else the fat would be in the proverbial fire. She had opened it and his signature was there with a short, standard Christmas message. But he had remembered, and her Christmas had been full of Parisian memories. She could almost feel his arms around her and the warmth of his last kiss.

"We need to get all these Christmas cards put away, Vikki," Dena said to her youngest daughter. "I'll start taking the decorations down."

"It was a great Christmas Mom. Did you enjoy it?"

"The best yet. Ah, there goes the phone."

"It for you. It's Aunt Angela."

"What does my sister want now?" she muttered taking the receiver. "Hello, Angie. Happy New Year"

"Dena. Yes, and the same to you all. Did you get my card?"

"Card? Now Angie you know that we agreed some years ago not to send cards," reminded Dena.

"Yes, I know darling, but I have started writing again and I took a day trip to Paris to get some ideas so I sent a card from there. I am writing under the old pseudonym 'Michel'. Remember darling…? Dena! Dena! Dena, are you there? Dena!"

The line had cleared. Strange, she thought as she slowly replaced the receiver.

18

19

The Boatyard Murder

He could sense that there was something wrong and hesitated to touch the light switch. The smell wasn't right; he shivered with fear of the unknown. Slowly his eyes were becoming accustomed to the darkness, and he recoiled from something nearby.

There was something moving, something awful and ugly. "My God! No!" Now he could see it. He could see the shape hanging just beside him. He could smell the dampness of his clothes. Forcing himself to pull the switch the horror of his imagination was confirmed before his eyes.

20

Of all mornings, Monday was Peter Smith's morning of 'the Black Dog'. The week-enders had left, leaving all their unwanted rubbish for him to dispose of. It was a daunting task for the most organised mind, and Peter didn't consider himself well blessed with this sort of acumen. His job as boatman at the local boat-yard covered everything under the sun and after a bank holiday weekend, other people's rubbish was his immediate concern.

At thirty five years of age Peter, an ex merchant navy seaman, had one personal attribute over and above those possessed by boatmen the world over. His countenance wore a permanent smile; a smile that spilled over into his watery eyes and gave confidence to those seeking maritime aid.

He wasn't normally a tidy person, but he hated disorganised chaos. He would only be happy when he had returned the yard to normality, allowing him to continue with his boatman's duties.

His first job, having unlocked the boat shed

doors, was to enjoy his daily cigarette, a luxury he had allowed himself since giving up smoking.

Feeling his way around the assortment of craft housed for repair, he had then made his way to the far corner of the darkened building, to the switch box. It was a corner he reserved for his own personal repair work.

Recovering from the immediate shock of finding a dead human, he could see that the body was that of the local rich guy, Tommy Mann. He was dead, of that there was little doubt. The body had been streaming with blood, which had dripped onto the floor.

Taking a closer look, Peter recognised his own personal marlinspike, a tool for managing difficult knots. It was protruding from the dead man's chest and had been driven in with some considerable force. Whoever had planted that, he thought, must have really meant it.

"I'll ring the police," said Willett, the boatyard owner, who made his appearance in response to Peter's telephone call. "Touch nothing Peter," Willett added. "I should wait outside until they arrive."

22

That sounds a good idea, thought Peter. A feeling of nausea had come over him and he had suddenly gone very cold. He had never experienced a hanging body before and, tough as he thought he was, this had been a shock.

Clumpton-on-sea wasn't a holidaymaker's paradise, quite the contrary; they were warned away. For some years the small beach had been invaded by scutch grass and the Parish Council had neither the will, nor the funds to deal with it.

Whilst the sea was clear and non-tidal, perfect for weekend bathers, it had hidden dangers. Signs were scattered around the beach warning of deep, hidden shelving inshore. The public were quick to realise that this feature, whilst a disaster for non-swimmers, was a godsend to yachtsmen, who were able to beach their vessels and load them onto their trailers with ease.

This natural phenomenon had needed little or no publicity. The weekend sailors had flocked in their numbers to the south coast, and Clumpton-on-sea had been ready and willing to receive them.

The two police cars arrived together and Inspector Thomas, CID, was first to the scene.

"Oh God, not poor old Tommy!" he said aloud, looking upwards at the corpse. "What a way to go. I always thought you would come to a sticky end."

"Now young man," said Thomas, turning to Peter with a questioning look, "tell me what you know about this lot."

Peter had seen too many who-don-its on the TV not to know what to say and what not to say.

"Ok. Hold it," said Thomas, noticing the procession of cars arriving - the police doc, photographers and the forensic guys. "Let's go into the boss's office."

"Now," continued Thomas, settling down in Willett's chair. "Who locked up last night?"

"I did, at about 6 pm. I locked the boathouse but didn't look inside," said Willett, having just arrived.

"Anybody about?"

"No. Everyone had…" started Willett.

"There was Mr Brown the flower-man, Mr Willett," interrupted Peter. "He puts flowers on the dogs' graves," he continued for Thomas's benefit.

"Ah yes, I'd forgotten," corrected Willett. "He uses the boatshed water for the flowers. He is very conscientious about locking up after finishing though."

"Hm… Peter," said Thomas with a thoughtful expression, "who has access to the pulley lift?"

"Most boat owners."

"Women?"

"Well, yes."

"And the spike that killed him?"

"Everyone that handles ropes."

"Where would it be found?"

"On my bench," replied Peter.

"Near the corpse?"

"Yes, just at the side."

"Hm…" Thomas was thoughtful. According to the doctor the time of death 8 pm Sunday. Forensic had little as yet but had taken the spike for examination. A picture was starting to take shape, but nothing definite.

"So John," said Thomas, arriving at the Garden Centre Entrance where John had come to meet him. "I presume the news has reached you?"

"Oh yes, sir. It's a very sad business," Brown replied. He was a good six feet three inches in height and standing with his arms folded was a picture of the local nightclub bouncer.

Thomas could see that this man knew his business. The sense of orderliness was apparent. Signs clearly identifying types of plants and shrubs made it easy for the customer to locate his needs. The paths were clean and tidy and the whole atmosphere of the business was welcoming.

26

"So, tell me about Sunday night at the boatyard," said Thomas after they had settled down in one of the conservatories.

"There is nothing much to tell Inspector. I only used the boat-house water tap for five minutes and then I left."

"Did you see any loiterers?" asked Thomas.

"No, just Mr Willett leaving and Peter popping back."

"Willett leaving. To go home presumably?" Thomas asked.

"Er… well no. He went the other way."

"For any reason you know of Mr Brown?"

"That, I don't know, Inspector."

"Ok. Now, what about Peter? Where did he get to?"

"Oh, he just closed the gates after me. You know, Inspector, there was no love lost between those two."

"Which two?"

" Peter and Mr Mann."

"Why was that?"

"Mann used to employ Peter as his office manager. He fired him for misconduct, refusing him any form of reference. And now the bastard is forcing his attentions on Mrs Willett."

Now then, thought Thomas, there's a thing. He could sense the feeling of hate rising in Brown's powerful body.

" So, I take it that there is no love lost between the dead man and Mrs Willett,"

"I wouldn't go so far as to say that, Inspector," said Brown toning down his voice.

"Well, what would you go so far as to say, Mr Brown?" He could see that the man was pulling back, as though he had said too much. "Was he being a nuisance to Mrs Willett?" tempted Thomas.

"I couldn't explain to you, Inspector, you wouldn't understand," said Brown, suddenly on the verge of tears.

Thomas could see that he had touched a raw spot. It was time to use a little tact. "I am sorry, Mr Brown. Would you like me to come back some other time?"

"No, no, no. Do excuse me." He sniffed and made a visible effort to pull himself together. Then, his emotions under control once more, explained, "It's just that our memories live so long. You see, many of us have lived in the village all our lives. We grew up together, sat together at the village school and prayed at the chapel together. I remember well how young Mann worshipped Mrs Willett, Edna Smart, as she was then. I don't think he has ever forgiven her for marrying Willett."

"Did he visit her without her husband's knowledge?" Thomas ventured, hoping that he might have found an opening.

"Nothing like that, Inspector, so far as I know," said Brown. "Now, please think, Mr Brown, did anything strange happen over the weekend?"

Brown lowered his head in thought before responding, "Not that I can recall, Inspector."

"Well, please call me if you do. Now, if I may," he asked, "I should like to speak with your wife?"

Whilst Thomas could picture Brown's brawny arms plunging that Marlin-spike into the dead man's chest, Mrs Brown hardly seemed capable of pushing a needle into an embroidery sampler. She was a gentle lady.

He had been provided him with a small trailer camper for an on-site office. A telephone had been connected and the furniture hirers had delivered a table and three chairs.

A strongly motivated local-man Thomas carried his forty-two years with increasing confidence on his well-trimmed frame. His dedication to the neighbourhood well-being had earned him respect among the locals that was the envy of his colleagues He sat reviewing his notes which contained an assortment of clues but nothing that really led anywhere

"So, Thomas, what have you got for me?" The Chief Inspector asked on a routine visit. In his day the chief had been the finest detective the force had ever known and, three years after his promotion to chief, it was apparent where his interest still lay.

"A lot of bits, sir," said Thomas. "I'll let you see them when they are sorted."

That was sufficient for the chief; he wasn't there to intrude. He left the Inspector to his thoughts.

Biting the end of his pencil Thomas wondered why Peter hadn't told him that he had returned to the yard after Willett had locked up. And why did Willett never go home on Saturdays after leaving the boatyard? He needed some quick answers from these unreliable witnesses.

Thomas's brain fed on activity, giving him a nervy disposition. His wiry frame, however, could handle all this, and more. It had to. He was a single parent family and his kids threw far more at him than his job could ever do.

Tonight was the PTA meeting at the kid's school and Thomas felt obliged to attend. Nikki, the elder of the two, was seven, a year and a half older than Tom who was the bright one in the family. He loved them both but that was still no compensation for the loss of his wife who had died producing Tom.

"...Evening Frank," the headmaster greeted Thomas as he took his place in one of the pupils' chairs. "I thought you would be too busy to attend this evening." He took a seat next to him. The head, liked to be present at all the PTA meetings, but never intruded into the discussions.

"It's the least I can do, headmaster," replied Thomas. "But anytime now the kids will know more than I do about some of these subjects."

"You'll have to go to night school," replied the head with a questioning look.

Thomas raised his eyebrows without comment. That would really be fun he thought.

Later that evening the kids were in bed and he was watching the late TV news. His conversation with the head on the subject of night school had reminded him of something. He was sure that Brown had a horticultural class on Monday nights, yet the man had made no mention of it and he would certainly have been too late to attend after he left the Garden Centre. Thomas grabbed for the phone. "Hello Mary-Jane. It's Frank Thomas here."

"Hi Frank, good to hear you. How is the enquiry going?"

"You know, Mary-Jane, a bit shitty at the moment."

Mary Jane had been the boss's secretary before she was forced to stop working to allow her to nurse her sick son. On top of all her other assets Mary Jane was a keen gardener.

"Did you go to class on Monday?" Thomas asked, hoping that he would solve the Brown problem at one fell blow.

"Yes, it was good, perhaps a little too technical for me."

"What about Brown. Was he teaching?"

"In fact he wasn't there. He just didn't turn up, which was strange for him. He usually sends an apology if he is unable to attend."

"Hum…"

"To do with the case, I presume," she added. "Say no more, Frank." She was the essence of tact, knowing not to ask unnecessary questions. "Keep in touch Mary-Jane. Thanks for your help," said Thomas, replacing the 'phone.

"So, Mr Brown. Where did *you* get to on Monday evening?" he said to himself.

Clumpton-on-sea, situated on the south coast, had few historic associations; no pirates or smugglers had visited its shores, that is, not until more recently, when cigarette smugglers from across the English Channel had been caught passing through the boatyard.

Offshore yachts or motor cruisers carrying the contraband from continental shores to the UK would heave-to a mile off the beach. Shore based craft would then casually take to the water and store the well-packed stock of cigarettes under their decks where it would be well hidden from sight until the boats joined the many craft in the boatyard, eventually to be towed away as normal week-end pleasure gear. By this means a million smokes were avoiding duty every week. But it only took one greedy boat owner to overload his boat, allowing a carton of cigarettes to be seen by the duty bobby. Customs and Excise were quick to act and thereafter included the area on its regular inspections.

"Now look here, laddie," Thomas demanded of Peter the following morning, "don't piss me about. You either left, or you didn't leave. Which was it? And I want the truth." He was hoping against hope that the boatman would provide some kind of a lead.

"I am sorry, Inspector, I didn't mean to mislead you," Peter replied." All I did was to return to the gate when I realised that the boss was coming out, save him getting out of his car."

" So you were the last to leave?"

" Yes," admitted Peter.

"See anyone hanging about? Now think lad, think bloody carefully."

Peter sat in a suspended state of animation for what, to Thomas, felt like minutes. He eventually spoke. "No, I can't remember seeing anyone."

"I don't bloody believe you," Thomas said, stomping away.

Someone was hiding something, of that he was sure. He wanted Brown sitting here right in front of him so that he could see the colour of his eyes.

"I think we can just run to a cup of tea, Mr Brown," the Inspector invited.

"I hope it's nothing serious, Inspector. I have left the business unattended. No, I don't want tea thanks."

Brown was a little nervous, a state of mind that pleased Thomas, perhaps he would now get some sense out of the man.

36

"Now, Mr Brown, you were saying at our last meeting that you had nothing further to report," said Thomas with an air of criticism. "Now, are you sure?"

Brown, feeling quite uncomfortable, sat opposite the Inspector in the cabin. He had chased down here feeling guilty as hell without need.

"Yes, I am quite sure, Inspector," he said in as short a tone as the situation would allow.

"What about the Customs officer?" asked Thomas. "I heard that he made a regular Sunday visit." It was a long shot, but he had to try everything.

"Customs? Oh, on Sunday you mean?"

"Yes, that's the day we are concerned with Mr Brown."

"Sunday?" Brown said to himself. "Oh yes, you mean Frank Jones. I'd forgotten. I am sorry, Inspector."

"Mr Brown," said Thomas in his best disciplinary voice. "It is an arrestable offence to withhold information, in addition to wasting police time. Now think,

Mr Brown, is there anything else you have forgotten to tell me?"

Brown sat motionless for a full minute, his head bowed as though in prayer. "I can honestly say, Inspector, that so far as I know there is nothing, and I am truly sorry about the Customs man."

"Right," said Thomas. "So tell me about Frank Jones, and I want everything. If I find you have missed anything, Brown, you are for the high jump."

"I am sorry to say, Inspector, there is nothing much to tell," Brown started.

"Let me be the judge of that, Brown. Please, carry on."

"Well, when I got back home from locking up with Peter, there was a telephone call from Frank Jones, the Customs and Excise man. He had heard from the coastguard that there was a boat approaching the shore and wanted to know if I would let him in the boatyard to check it. I told him that it wasn't convenient at that moment but I could come in about half an hour's time."

"Hadn't he got a key?" asked Thomas, listening intently to the unfolding story whilst turning the pages of his pad.

" No. Mr Willett about issuing keys. He keeps a strict record of all key holders."

"Ok. So what happened then?"

"Well, it was quite strange. When I arrived at the boatyard for the second time the Customs man was waiting at the gate. But it wasn't Frank Jones. It was someone I'd never seen before. He said Frank had sent him. He was dressed in the Customs outfit all right and showed me his pass so I let him in and showed him how to lock the gate when he left."

"Right, Brown, before you go any further, when did you return to check that the gate had been made secure for the night?"

"Seven-thirty pm," replied Brown.

"How do you know that?" asked the Inspector, checking his notes.

"I was watching the TV and I left a few minutes before the end of Gardener's World, which finishes at seven thirty pm."

"Was the gate locked?"

"Yes, everywhere was secure."

"And you didn't observe anything else? You would have been there very near to the time of the murder."

"No Inspector. I went straight back home in time to see the start of the news at seven forty-five pm."

"How do you suggest I try to trace this Customs official?" asked Thomas. "Did you check to see if he came from the Clumpton office?"

"No, I just presumed that he had," was the reply.

"Right. Perhaps you could give me a detailed description of him? Just complete this form with as much information as you can remember." He shoved a forma across the desk and then sat back and waited.

A little later he called in at the station. He needed information.

"Hey, Inspector," shouted the sexy telephone operator as he entered the office, " been overdrawing again, naughty boy. The bank is on the blower."

He couldn't help smiling to himself, but he wished she wouldn't do it.

The bank manager told him that the boatyard was in deep financial trouble. Thomas replaced the receiver wondering where that piece of information would take him. Peter was hiding something, as was Brown of the Garden Centre. The only person in the clear at the moment was Willett. But neither Peter nor Brown were involved enough to be concerned with the financial side of the business.

Mann's death hadn't been an accident, that much was sure, so it had to have been the action of someone who was deeply worried. But worried about what? He answered his own question. It could only be money.

41

He telephoned the Customs office in Clumpton. The chief vouched for the stranger, explaining that Frank Jones had been redirected to the airport.

"There is nothing showing on the spike," said the forensic officer. "He must have worn gloves."

"What kind of gloves?" snapped Thomas. The useless buggers, he thought. There had to be something showing, if only blood.

"Plastic it suggests here. But I see we found a short fibre, that we suspect is of far eastern origin," the man said nervously

Sailing gloves, Thomas thought to himself. He remembered Peter saying that the village chandlery shop supplied all their needs. It could be worth a visit. "I could do with some sailing gloves," Thomas told the assistant at the chandlery shop.

He was presented with two types, both with rubber palms.

"These are our favourites," explained the assistant. "You see the rubber insert provides a much firmer grip.

Yes, he could see that, but it wasn't what he was looking for. He was beginning to think that he wasn't going to find what he needed.

"Are these all that you stock," Thomas asked.

"I am afraid so, sir. We have never stocked other types."

"I would have thought gloves were chandlery to a sailor, Peter?" he said later. "Yes, I am sure you are right, Inspector. But recently the yard received a couple of sample pairs from abroad. They were much cheaper."

"Presumably with rubber palms?" Thomas asked

"No, they were not that type,"

"What happened to them?" queried Thomas.

"Well, the boss ordered a supply."

Good, thought Thomas, his spirits beginning to rise again. "Let's have a look at them, Peter."

43

"But, you can't," answered Peter. "You see, Mrs Willett buys all the gloves and when they arrived the C.O.D price was wrong, and she sent them all back."

His heartbeat stopped, another dead-end. "So you haven't had any imported gloves yet?" he asked, turning to leave. He got to the boathouse doors. "If you think of anything, Peter…"

"We still have the sample gloves, " called Peter, delving into his pocket. "Here are mine."

Hastening back to Peter, he took the gloves, which were battered and torn. "Pretty well knackered aren't they? I'll borrow them for a while if I may, Peter?"

"Ok. Sorry about the condition. They do get a lot of use."

"Where are the others, Peter?" he asked. Peter shrugged. "I don't know. You will have to ask Mrs Willett, Inspector."

"Well, what do you think about these?" said Thomas producing the gloves for the forensic officer.

"Ah, struck lucky, eh Inspector? Let's take a look."

The Forensic Laboratory always left him with the shivers.
"Take a look Inspector," said the forensic guy to Thomas.
"Is it all right?" questioned Thomas.
"Yes, take a look."
He put his eye to the lens and could clearly see the enlarged samples of woollen thread.
"…but they are not the same," remarked Thomas.
"No," said the forensic officer in deep thought.
Thomas stood motionless, anxious not to disturb his colleague's train of thought.
"All other factors like gauge and structure agree with the exception of colour. I am sorry to disappoint you again Inspector, but it isn't a match."

The station was busy. There had been a scare on. A customs raid on a landing beach party. The DI's were briefing their men and he looked for somewhere to sit but the chief had seen him and waved for him to join him.

"Well Inspector. What progress?"

He explained about the forensic tests and how he had hoped that he was onto something, but the tests proved negative.

"You say two out of three, that sounds an good average Thomas. I shouldn't be disappointed. I wouldn't be surprised if you find that it is something staring you in the face."

Never negative, the man was a jewel; issuing confidence when needed but quick to correct the over zealous.

The chief was right the answer had got to be just waiting to be seen.

Peter was down in the boat-park working on an outboard engine, they said.

"I'll not forget to return your gloves Peter," Thomas said walking into the repair shed. Intrigued with the deftness of the man, he could turn his hand to virtually any mechanical defect.

"No problem," replied Peter, anxious to know the state of the inquiry but afraid to ask.

"Were the sample gloves all the same colour?" Thomas asked.

"So far as I know Inspector, of course I only saw the one pair," Peter replied with a questioning look. "Why, is there some problem about colour?"

Anxious not to allow the boatman to become too involved, "No, just a query."

"What's the smell in here Peter?" asked Thomas sniffing around the shed.

"Oh, it's that engine coolant liquid in the can," Peter replied pointing to a large can of green liquid. "One of the boat owners has a private aircraft and he asked me look at the engine. It needed its coolant topping up and that is the remains.

"Strange stuff," said the Inspector taking a final sniff on his way out.

Walking back to the boatshed he was met by Mr Willet.

"You are wanted on the 'phone, Inspector," he said. "Please use my office."

"Many thanks," answered Thomas.

He was just about to break into a trot, when…

"Inspector! Inspector!" It was Peter chasing after him.

" I have a call Peter."

"This is important Inspector. Wait!" he called.

Indeed Peter was right it was important.

Returning the excess aircraft coolant to the repair shed, Peter's gloves had accidentally fallen into the green ethylene glycol. He hadn't noticed them until the following morning, when he recovered them from the can and put them on the radiator to dry. Later he did notice that they had taken on a different colour.

Forensic was able to test a small sample of thread taken from the marlinspike. They had found a match.

Mrs Willett opened her front door and greeted him with a smile. " Hello Inspector. Please come in."

He was invited into the living room, which looked the essence of comfort and showed for the loving care that was regularly lavished upon it

"May I get you a coffee, whiskey, sherry?"

"Oh no, Mrs Willett, I've just had coffee and I very rarely take strong liquor on duty."

"In that case Inspector I should explain that my husband is in the yard."

"Oh yes, I realise that Mrs Willett. It was you that I wished to speak to."

"In that case, what can I do for you?" she said, settling herself into a comfortable armchair.

"I have just a few questions I should like to ask in connection with the sad business involving Mr Mann." He felt a little embarrassed at having to mention the subject to such a lovely lady.

"Yes, I understand Inspector, please carry on."

"Well, I'm interested in the sample gloves that you received from abroad. We have the pair you gave to

Peter but I just wondered if you had retained the other?"

He saw at once that the words meant something to her.

"I don't usually keep unwanted things about Inspector, and I can't be certain what I did with them. I'll have a good look for them and let you know. Will that be alright?"

"Yes, yes of course. Perhaps you would call in at the office and let me know?"

"By all means Inspector, as soon as possible."

Facial expressions were a Thomas's speciality and Mrs Willett's face told the story that he wanted to know.

It had been a dull miserable day with low cloud and darkness fell early. Hidden by the deepening shadows an unannounced caller stole through the wicket gate and crept around the back of the Willett house. He could see that the rubbish hadn't been collected.

He worked quietly and carefully trying not to disturb the household. After trawling through the remains of the Willett's menus for the past week he stopped, and then he smiled to himself. It was a smile of success; he had found what he was looking for. Carefully refilling the waste bins, he dusted himself down and left as stealthily as he had come.

"I wondered who had been interested in our rubbish, Inspector. I should have known."

Thomas had called as soon as he had seen Willett leave for his office. The sight of the plastic bag containing the gloves was enough for the lady of the house.

"I wondered how long it would be before you came across something incriminating," she sighed. "I thought the rubbish had been collected."

"May I come in," he asked.

"Yes, of course" she said, leading him into the sitting room.

"The gloves let me down, but it doesn't matter. I've reached the end of my tether. Did you know the bastard was going to foreclose on Henry? We should have never taken his loan in the first place. As if that wasn't bad enough, the minute Henry left to see his mother every Sunday; he was here pestering me, forever pestering me. I hated the man." Her voice was turning into a scream. "Yes, I hated the man. He just wouldn't bloody leave me alone. I hated the bloody man." Now she was screaming at the top of her voice.

He now knew how the marlinspike had pierced the fat body of Tommy Mann. Now he understood the power of a woman defiled.

"I had had enough," she said in a quiet controlled voice. "I am sorry I tried to mislead you, Inspector."

Thomas nodded, and stood up, strangely reluctant to start the formalities. He hadn't come to arrest her; he had just been checking on the gloves. But a confession would be cheaper for the taxpayer, and might even help her in the long run.

52

53

Vin l'mour

Hanging around airports is no fun, thought Henry. There's got to be a better way of spending a Saturday afternoon. He was waiting, along with a thousand others, for flights to various European destinations. But they were not going anywhere. Fog had closed most of the Mediterranean resorts and was showing no sign of lifting.

Gradually the number of people was slowly reducing, but not to take-off. Flight numbers were being announced to tell passengers to report to the coach park for transport to a local hotel for the night.

Henry had taken a short golfing holiday to prepare him for the coming season. It hadn't been possible to play at home; incessant rain had closed the greens at most clubs, and the forward weather forecast hadn't given any hope for drier weather.

He was 28 years of age, a little over 6 feet in height and of slim build. His hazel eyes matched his auburn hair, which was in a modern style, adding to his good looks. Barbara, his wife, would be expecting a call just now, he thought, to collect him from the UK airport.

Hotel Calla Blanca was situated facing the beach. It had been built of breeze- block, rendered and then finished in local colours, pink and white. The entrance was inviting, particularly to those who had been anticipating a night spent spread out on two chairs at the airport. It couldn't pretend to be an imposing structure as it was partially hidden in the sand dunes, but to this crowd it a welcoming haven for the night.

The fog was less dense here but Henry could see that the sand had drifted everywhere. The gardens and paving were covered in sand; it was even finding its way into the entrance porch where it was kept at bay by a number of grills set into the floor. An attempt had been made to preserve a small south facing, tabled area with a glazed awning, allowing drinks to be taken outside.

Having passed through the foyer into the main reception area Henry felt satisfied that the accommodation would fit the purpose for which it was intended. He quickly checked his luggage, inspected his room and retired to the bar.

There were already a host of nationalities present, French, German and now British, all clamouring for drinks. The lady in front of Henry was struggling to make herself heard in French, but he could see that she wasn't succeeding.

"Pardon, Mademoiselle. May I help?" he asked.

"Ah, oui Monsieur, merci," she replied turning to greet him with a smile. "The bar is busy."

"Yes it is. Have you been waiting long?"

"Quite some time," she responded, looking at her watch.

"Let me help, Madam." Henry withdrew her from the crowed bar and called a waiter from nearby. "I thought perhaps, Madam, that you would like to join me in a glass of wine or other aperitif, say in the foyer or on the porch?"

She hesitated, as though taken aback. "That is kind of you. Yes, a glass of wine would be nice," she agreed eventually.

Henry then turned to the waiter. After enquiring after the house wine he decided on a wine of his own choice.

"We should like to take a bottle of wine at a table in the conservatory area," he said to the waiter.

"I have ordered a wine of your country, which I am sure you will like. If not we shall try another," he said, taking her arm and leading her out of the crowded room.

Reaching the foyer Henry hesitated. "My name is Henry Bollington. I am returning to England after a week's golf in Palma. I hope you don't think I am being forward but I thought it would be better to be away from the bar area."

"Thank you, Henry," she said accepting his explanation. "Yes, perhaps we did have a rather rude introduction amongst the crowds in the other room, but it is better in here. Thank you again, my name is Helen and I am returning to Paris following a visit to Palma on business."

It was quieter outside and with the help of the wine they found it easy to converse. They talked of Paris, London and Palma and back to Paris as she explained the reason for her visit to Palma. He discovered that she was a graphic designer with Paris Match, the up market magazine, and had been to Palma to meet advertisers.

Suddenly they realised that it was time to prepare for dinner.

"Please join me for dinner, Helen," Henry asked. "It is a boring business dining alone. Don't you agree?"

"Yes, I am sure you are correct," she said, carefully considering his invitation." If you were sure that I wouldn't be intruding then, yes, that would be pleasant. Thank you."

Well, thought Henry, taking a cold shower, what a lovely woman. He couldn't believe that after such a boring afternoon he should meet with such a charming person. She was everything he expected from a Parisian lady of quality. She had that slight Algerian look that made the ladies of Paris so special. He had noticed the attractive birthmark nearly hidden in the texture of her delicate complexion. Her well-styled hair accentuated her medium height and slim figure and her dress, of a delicate blue chiffon, added style to her ensemble. A light, matching coat thrown over her shoulders completed her attire.

Surprisingly, the restaurant had a pleasant décor. They were late and the unoccupied tables were few but the headwaiter, as though understanding their wishes, found them a table away from the main seating area.

"Would you like to choose the wine, Helen?" he asked.

"I should prefer that you did, Henry. I liked your earlier choice."

"Would you like French or German or …" he started, glancing through the wine list.

"Let's have your previous choice, Henry. If you agree," she said with a smile.

They made their choices from the menu and returned to discussing their respective lives.

Both were happily married with young children and had very demanding business lives. A chance meeting such as this wasn't part of the normal routine for either of them. She lived in Neuilly and travelled into the city daily by car. Her husband was a senior partner in a busy city

Architects. Their children were still at local schools and were cared for in the daytime by a housekeeper.

Having finished their meal they realised that the restaurant was empty. A sense of quiet had descended on the hotel.

They left their table and casually strolled together into the foyer where they sat for a while admiring the décor and wall decorations, continuing there discussions. And then, as though with one mind, they walked to the entrance and saw that the misty atmosphere was keeping the air warm and enticing. Wandering out into the sand dunes they went arm in arm along the edge of the sea, looking eerie in the ghostly atmosphere.

He put his arm around her waist to steady their steps over the uneven sand and then, quite suddenly, as though someone with mystic powers had waved a wand, the fog was gone and the scene had changed.

They wandered over to the sand dunes where blades of grass were just starting to show through the sand.

Holding her gently he kissed her. He could feel her soft warm, petite body through her silky dress as he caressed the gentle slopes of her waist and enjoyed the pressure of her firm breasts.

They folded together onto the sand between the dunes and he could feel her slender legs through her sheer stockings. She felt his fingers stroking her gently, reawakening the fires inside her. She closed her eyes. She felt his lips brushing her flesh and heard the soft sounds of pleasure when he raised his lips from hers.

An expression of almost frightening ecstasy came onto his face as she felt the trembling deep within her. From what deep feeling could such pleasure come? It was an almost unbearable delight, like nothing she had ever known before?

She whispered, "Henry, my love."

"Darling," was his only response.

They lay there together, their thoughts forever linked to that moment of sheer ecstasy they had shared. He held her close in his arms, telling her of his love for her.

And then came that first movement back to normality. He kissed her, adjusted her dress and they both stood, together, in one another's arms.

"Mon ami, I shall never forget this moment," she whispered with a deep French accent.

"Nor I my love," he replied.

They strolled back to the hotel locked in one another's arms until it was time to part. This was their last private moment. They looked deep into each other's eyes as though held by some hidden attraction. Then they kissed, and they parted.

The coaches were here. Early morning breakfast had been arranged and they were leaving within the hour.

Milling people and cases filled the hotel. The lifts were full and the stairs cluttered with people and luggage.

"She has to be amongst these hundreds of people," Henry said to himself, but fate decided otherwise.

They never met again, but they remembered.

It was a bright sunny morning and Euston station looked its best with crowds crossing the entrance foyer.

"Barbara. I think we need something to read for the journey," Henry said to his wife as they passed the news-stand."

"Yes darling, but let's get into our seats first."

Barbara Bollington was tall and slim with colouring much as her husband, fair with blue eyes. She carried herself with an elegant poise and looked every inch a lady of quality. In fact Barbara came from stock slightly higher up the social scale than her husband but ignoring that, they were a happily matched couple.

They were on their way with the children to visit Barbara's brother in Edinburgh. Henry had reserved their seats and they were quick to locate them and deposit their luggage.

"Now kids, what do you want to read?" Henry asked.

"Henry, please!" Barbara reacted.

"Sorry darling. Children," Henry corrected.

"We have our reading thank you, Dad," the children replied in unison.

"And, my darling, what about you?"

"I will leave it to you, something arresting," she replied with a giggle.

"Whow!" said Henry. "Leave it to me, my love."

What an array of rubbish, he thought at the newsstand. Women's mags left him cold He picked a golfing magazine for himself and continued looking for Barbara. The variety was extensive; you were certainly spoiled for choice. He was on the point of deciding when his eyes caught sight of a front cover photograph. A familiar face, he thought. He looked closer and noticed the name Paris Match. "God!" he said aloud. "It's her, Helen." He stopped and looked again it couldn't be true, but yes it was true enough. It was Helen. The blazoned headline said, **"The love I once had - see page 23."**

"God no!" Henry repeated. It can't be. He found the page and read the first few lines.

He heard the signal; the train was leaving. He had to get that magazine. He grabbed at it off the rack left his money and flew.

The train had started to move but the carriage was nearby and Henry leisurely opened the door and stepped on board.

"You left it a little late, darling," said Barbara observing her husband with an armful of magazines and newspapers.

"I am sorry I was so long. There is such an array of magazines these days it is difficult to choose," he said placing the dailies on the seat and the magazines on the rack.

"Oh, Henry dear, did I catch a glimpse of Paris Match?" asked Barbara. "My word, you have been splashing out."

"Yes, I thought it would be a change from the usual UK stuff," said Henry, passing the magazine to his wife.

66

They had just taken on passengers at Crewe and Henry noted that his wife had been reading her magazine solidly all the way from Euston. He wandered what could be so engaging. Suddenly, she took his arm and with a long sigh she rested her head on his sleeve.

"Oh Henry, that was a lovely article." He caught sight of the page, which carried a small picture of Helen. "I wonder if it is true; she writes so knowingly," she said, taking her handkerchief to her eyes." It reminded me of us when we were young," she whispered tightening her grip on her husband's arm.

Helen had recounted their hour of love making with tenderness and affection, changing names and places, but he was happy that she had returned his love in such a way.

The Trip

He couldn't understand where all this mystery regarding computers had come from They just computed, calculated or worked-out. In fact the Romans had had them, and the Ancient Brits. A tin box, a few printed circuits a chip and you'd got it.

With his head inside the computer Angus Smelzter was trying out an experiment. He was sure he could increase its power if he could adjust the inside a little.

He was ten years old and was already well on the way to designing his own computer. He had been born on the very day that the Prime Minister had announced the coming of a new age. The age of the Electronic Airwave.

He took his screwdriver and directed it towards a screw in the modem. There was a small thump and a flash. All the house lights went out.

"Angus," shouted his mother from downstairs, "what are you doing?"

"Nothing Mum," was his apologetic response. He looked around. What could he do to put the lights on again? He had probably blown the main fuse.

"Angie dear, what *are* you doing? You've fused the lights and I have a cake in the oven."

"Hello Angus," said a voice nearby.

"What did you say Mum?" shouted Angus. He couldn't move as he couldn't see where to move to.

"I'll have to go down the street to get the electrician. Now don't do anything stupid whilst I am out. Just leave things alone."

"Hello Angus," repeated the voice

"What was that?" Angus whispered to himself. The bedroom was dark he could just see the outline of the window.

"I'm here. Angus."

Delicately coaxing his head out of the back of the computer Angus looked around.

"Oh God! Mum! Mum!" he shouted, just as he heard the unmistakable sound of the front door closing behind her. "Don't go yet. Wait for me." He made for where he though the door should be and blundered into the wardrobe.

"It's alright, Angie. I'm not here to harm you," the voice said. "Please don't go."

Angus saw a glowing figure at the corner of the table. It was not unpleasant to look at and had the aroma of a delicate perfume. Everything about it seemed to be normal, but its head was flattened, giving it a wide mouth and stabbing, glass-like eyes. Most strangely of all, everything about it glowed in colours of the rainbow. Its presence cast a faint glow over the room.

Strange, Angus thought, it speaks without moving its mouth. It was carrying what looked to be a metal case in its left hand.

"Where did you come from?" Angus asked, trying to stay calm.

"Well, where do you think, Angus? Have a guess?"

"Have a guess?" repeated Angus. "I couldn't...I wouldn't know..." He was still a little uncertain what to do. Should he make a dash for it to the stairs, and out of the house?

"Take a wild guess," encouraged the apparition.

He didn't want to guess, in fact he wanted it to go away, and yet, at the same time there was something pleasant about it, something that he liked. It was quiet and gentle, and smiled all the time. Perhaps it could be a friend.

"You look like someone from outer space," volunteered Angus, though he had never experienced an apparition like this before.

"Now there you see, you guessed right first time."

"And why are you here?" asked Angus. He had heard of these happenings, but usually they were attributable to ghosts, and ghosts couldn't be seen like this, of that he was sure.

"Let me introduce myself, Angus," said the apparition. He must take great care not to speak of his mission to earth from his home planet Uranus, where life was threatened due to the absence of a brain. The box he carried was the brain that gave signals to the rest of his image but all the boxes were failing; they were worn out and soon the planet would be without life.

"Bring back the brain of a young boy," his master had instructed him, adding, "This was the last opportunity to save our planet."

"My name is Koy and you have called me from a

distant planet to be your friend."

"I didn't call you," retorted Angus angrily. "How could I?" He had noted how the shape bowed forward and backwards as it spoke.

"Oh yes you did," insisted Koy.

"But how? How did I call you?" Angus persisted. He couldn't recall having done anything that would bring someone from outer space.

"Ah, Angus, I must explain," Koy replied. "You see, your computer modem is powerful in itself. Its power is 25,000 bytes but when you shorted the terminals with your screwdriver you squared that number to give many million bytes. The signal was week and the power small but it reached our planet and it was our duty to respond."

"Is your planet warm and pretty?" asked Angus, forgetting his fear and getting interested now. He had always seen pictures of bleak landscapes and steaming wastelands, he was sure that they couldn't be true.

"But of course," said Koy, his mouth writhed into a smile. "The sun always shines, the grass is always green and the flowers never die. It is like what earth people call heaven. There are no wars like you have here, nor are there any disagreements."

Sounds a little strange, though Angus. "What about computers?" he asked. "Do you know about them?"

"We have known about computers since the birth of our planet," said Koy. "They decide everything. What and when we eat. Where we live and work. When we wake and when we sleep, even when we live and when we die."

Koy could see the incredulous expression on the face of the boy; he was saying too much.

"But can't you decide things for yourself?" asked Angus looking worried.

"There is nothing to stop us from disobeying," said Koy, " but if you do you are liable to being taken off the electronic mailing lists."

"What happens then?" asked Angus.

"You will just wither away because you will receive no food or water."

"What do you mean?" asked Angus. Wither away? He didn't like the sound of that.

"Well, our bodies are so constructed that they need regular inputs of food and water to survive. Without this nourishment the body shrivels and dies. All that remains is a few particles of dust."

Angus was speechless. He took a closer look at Koy's body. It was difficult to see....

"Angus," his mother interrupted their conversation." The electrician wasn't there but they are going to send him when he returns. I'll bring you a candle."

"All right, mother," replied Angus.

"A candle?" said Koy with a strong note of concern. "What is a candle?"

"It is a light, to make the room brighter,"

"Yes," said Koy. "But what kind of a light?"

"A flame."

The beautiful rainbow colouring of Koy's body suddenly turned dark grey. Its forward and backward movement changed to a rapid reverberation and Angus detected a foul smell coming from Koy's direction.

"What is the matter?" he asked. But Koy had disappeared.

"Here's your candle," said Angus's mother walking into the room with large brass candlestick carrying an equally large candle. "You will be able to see what you are doing now. By the way, what are you doing?" she asked, eyeing him suspiciously.

"Nothing much, Mum. I'll tell you later."

As soon as his mother had gone downstairs, Angus blew out the candle and called quietly for Koy.

"Koy. Where are you?" he whispered.

"I am here, Angus," whispered Koy, slowly reappearing at the corner of the table.

"Why did you leave, Koy? There is no need to be afraid of a candle."

"I am afraid there is, Angus," replied Koy. "You see our skin is like the wings of a moth and burns very easily. We have to keep very clear of naked flames."

"Oh, I see," said Angus. "I'm sorry."

He heard some noises downstairs. Presumably the electrician had arrived. He called down to his mother but she didn't hear him.

Koy was getting a little anxious. Time was running out on him. He needed a calorie input and he was no nearer to getting 'the brain of a young boy,'

"I think you would enjoy a visit to my land, Angus." He made it sound a casual invitation

"Oh, I couldn't do that, Koy. Mum wouldn't allow it."

"But Mum need not know,"

"How could you do that, Koy? My mother knows everything."

"In space, time has no measure. You would return at the same time as when you left."

"Oh!" Now that was something he didn't know. "How can you do that?" he asked, impressed.

"In space everything stops," said Koy. "Sound and movement are the only functions that continue."

"Would I have chance to see some of your computers and talk to the men that make them," asked Angus. That would be a feather in his cap. The smart Alecs in his class would have a shock when he told what he had seen.

"I am sure that you would be able to see all kinds of computers and the men that build them. So, would you like to go now, Angus?"

"I'll just go downstairs and ask Mum if it is all right."

"No, no, no. You must not do that," said Koy. He was beginning to give up on this lad, he had wasted too much precious time with him and he was no nearer to getting his brain. "It is possible to visit my home," suggested Koy as an additional incentive, "just for a short time to see for yourself."

He could be back before the lights came on, thought Angus, and what a wonderful experience he would have had. It was an opportunity too wonderful to miss.

"Are you sure that I would be back at the same time as I leave," he asked, looking for some form of reassurance.

"I promise," said Koy with a sheepish grin. He had no feelings of remorse. Truth and lies were just the same to him. In fact on his planet black was white, and dark was light. There were no rules, no laws. They were fed each day from a central computer, and they lived for a while and then they ceased to exist.

"Then let's do it," Angus said.

Koy was having second thoughts. He couldn't take this young boy away from everything he knew. His ignorance would be a liability. And yet he had the human brain that his planet badly needed. He must do as his masters required.

"So Angus, when you are ready, hold tight," said Koy, reaching for Angus's hand. "Off we go."

"Plop." The lights were on.

"Angus," shouted his mother. "Have you been sitting on your own in the dark all this time?"

"No... er...yes. I'm all right, mum. Thanks for the lights."

There was no sign of Koy. He looked around the table where he had stood but there was nothing. Angus had almost decided that he must have been dreaming but then ... The perfume! He could just detect that faint perfumey smell that Koy had left behind.

80

The Angel of Mercy

It had been a year of planning with every spare minute accounted for in the run up to the start of the race, and now *The Pride of Menai,* a 12 metre Beneteau racing yacht, looked every inch a winner. Every shackle had been checked, every sheet tested, halyards, lines and all the working gear had been checked and double-checked; it was too late now to find anything seriously wrong. There were twenty-four hours to go to the start of the single-handed Trans-Atlantic Yacht Race.

Ashore, the Royal Yacht Squadron clubhouse in Cowes was ablaze with lights. Sailing Instructions had been read and re-read, and now a hundred and twenty skippers bought the last drinks for their wives, girl friends and crews, all wishing to share in the excitement.

The weather forecast was mixed, giving a deep low pressure accompanied by heavy rain showers, with wind force 3 to 4, Northwest by west. A little north is always good, said Alex to himself, stroking his thin auburn moustache, but please God, no stronger.

Alex Worthington was a seasoned yachtsman. At 38 years of age he had over twenty years of sailing under his belt. Chairman of his own engineering company he had been introduced to the local sailing club in the Midlands by one of the company's employees. It had been real aggressive dinghy racing where rules had to be fully understood to survive. A wonderful family club where barristers argued waterborne infringements with low-paid manual workers, stimulating personal relationships that would remain throughout their lives

The sea was the problem. He ached to sail on the expansive sea, to do battle with the elements, to dice with the tides and, above all, to go foreign.

For the last ten years he had been a member of a well-known south coast club whilst still retaining his membership at home. During this time boats had come and gone but he had been fortunate in retaining a young, keen crew. Between them they had won most of the honours of the club and had started looking around for pastures new.

At that time single-handed yacht racing was the furthest thing from his mind. He considered it to be an unsociable pastime and preferred the teamsmanship of his crew, relishing their reactions to crisis and their different personalities. But then, it had happened. He had watched the start of the first single-handed race and watching those boats disappear down the Solent was all he needed. He had been sold.

The start in the Solent had been well disciplined, but now the fleet of boats were headed west down the English Channel and, having connected the self steering gear, Alex was able to observe the lights of the French coast slowly disappearing astern. They were approaching the Atlantic with its larger and more ominous looking seas.

The rain hadn't ceased all day and the wind strength had increased to force 5 with little north in its direction. The rest of the fleet had scattered and having set a course that would take him a hundred miles south of the others, Alex was aware that by morning he would be alone, ploughing through these ever increasing seas on his way to the Azores.

He had re-checked all deck gear, ropes, cleats, winches and self steering gear, a feature without which this race wouldn't have been born. With heavier weather forecast ahead, he decided that he would catch a short sleep. His bunk was covered with a waterproof and being located amidships he wouldn't feel the movement of the boat too much.

Conditions were worsening. He had left the Azores to starboard some hundred and fifty nautical miles astern. Briefly he had toyed with the idea of putting into port and calling it a day, but had immediately discarded the idea. Since then it had been three days of battling with the elements. Daylight had been scarce in the last thirty-six hours and the low black cloud ceiling had driven the wind velocity up to gale force eight on the Beaufort scale, with heavy rain showers. He was reefed down to the minimum to maintain some control. It wasn't yacht racing any longer; it was survival. The noise of the seas driven by the gale was frightening. The wind was driving the hull up the thirty foot waves until the forward half of the boat was clear of the wave crest, only to crash down and slide down the back of the wave, in readiness for ploughing into the next.

"God, how long can a boat survive this?" he said aloud as he sat at the chart table, checking his course. It was necessary to hear a voice if only his own. The radio was a godsend; he had reached the stage were he was conversing with the disc jockeys.

He prayed. He wasn't a religious man but agreed with the supreme being theory and in his short life there had been times when he had need to call on his maker.

He bowed his head. "Oh God, your seas are so large and my boat so small, have mercy on me."

Race Control had said that he was receiving the worst of the gale. He was on the edge of a deep depression which would run out in two or three days. In the meanwhile he would just have to sit it out.

Below decks everything was reasonably secure, his navigation equipment locked in a watertight drawer. The bilge pumps, struggling to cope with the rising water level, needed assistance from a hand pump. Sleep had deserted him for the last two days and he had given himself a pep pill to keep awake.

The reefed sails were doing their job satisfactorily, forcing the boat forward at a reasonable speed. This comforted him as above all things he needed to maintain his position amongst the fleet

Then suddenly, without any warning: Crash! Bang! The hull lifted into the air like a toy balloon and then slowly, giving him just enough time to adjust his position, it rolled onto its side. He waited for her to recover, bracing himself as she returned to her upright position. But it didn't happen. Now he sensed that the motion was different. There was no longer any sense of the boat driving itself forward. She was just a waterlogged hulk, bobbing up and down the waves.

Cautiously making his way out of the cabin, securing his harness as he went, he could see the cause of the capsize. The self steering gear had been carried away and rudder control had gone. He could only wait and pray that the boat would right itself, and slowly his prayer was answered. The mast began to emerge from the boiling sea, struggling with the waterlogged sails still attached to it. He grabbed the tiller to steer the boat back onto its course. But there was another terrifying crack, followed by a tearing, crashing sound. "Christ! "Whatever was that?" he said aloud. Then, without any warning, his world went black.

He immediately realised what had happened. The weight of water in the submerged sails had been too much for the mast. It had weakened and buckled. But, in continuing to right itself to the vertical position, the mast had met the unsparing power of the wind. It had broken at the hounds, halfway up the mast, collapsing and engulfing the vessel in sails and rigging. For him, the race was over.

His first action was to send the Mayday signal, alerting International Rescue Services and giving his location. He then set about recovering the broken mast rigging, clipping on his harness each time he moved. The gale persisted and working in these conditions left cuts and gashes in his hands, added to which the continued wave pattern was making him seasick. And then he realised what was actually happening.

The boat was sinking! No longer a responsive animal ploughing through the seas and driven by the wind, the stationary hulk was being swamped and the bilge pump had no hope of coping with the water. He turned quickly to the life raft, eased it from its cradle and prepared it for inflation.

The launching of the bell shaped raft had automatically set off a beacon signal, advertising his position, so he was a little more than disappointed when, after three days, he had seen no evidence of rescue.

The waterlogged hull, now drifting aimlessly, had disappeared from sight and he was alone in the boiling ocean. He had rationed the food and water, using only half the recommended ration. The wind dropped a little, allowing him to open the door flap of the bell, which he quickly closed again when a rogue wave swamped the raft.

It was 2 am. on his eighth day when his sleep was disturbed by the screech of a seagull. He opened the flap and there she was perched on the raft surround, as white as the driven snow. He could spare a crumb, he thought. Snowy appeared daily for her crumb and she had allowed him to secure a message ring around her leg giving his approximate compass bearing and the date. Futile he thought, being a thousand miles from the nearest land.

He was now down to the last of his food with three days of water left and still the seagull came every day. It was for her that he opened his eyes in the morning but he was weak now, sodden and chilled to numbness. His fingers weren't working properly and he had accidentally lost the flares through the doorway. They had floated away and he hadn't the will to swim after them.

He had lost count of the days, had stopped at fifteen. He was sleeping more now. Thank God the weather had eased.

It was on a beautiful morning, three days later, that paramedic was lowered into the water from the hovering helicopter. Tearing open the flap he looked inside the raft to see the half swamped body of a man floating inside. Taking his radiotelephone from his pocket he spoke to the pilot, "Hello Bill, another stiff."

Quickly hooking the shape onto his harness he gave the signal and, watched by the seagull, he was winched clear.

Once they had been winched on board he bent briefly over his charge and confirmed, "He *is* dead," to his pilot. Just then an eyelid flickered. "No Bill, there's life there," he shouted. "Press on. We are going to win this one for a change."

He looked down towards the life raft and saw that a white seagull was just leaving the life raft, returning to her current abode, MV. Atlantic Conveyor, three days out of Los Angeles bound for Cape Town.

Jacques le Merc.

Reversing his car out of the garage as he had done so many times before he was careful to avoid any obstructions that would mark the gleaming bodywork of his pride and joy. The margins for error were small and he dared not think of the cost of removing the smallest blemish.

Jacques Le Pretre had entered a new phase of life. His slightly portly frame ignored his fifty years of age and he had convinced himself that the best was yet to come with his new Mercedes.

The villagers had suffered a similar fate; the car had become a symbol of prestige and they were bound to acknowledge it as it passed by. It was the subject of conversation throughout the province, and now the local press had extended the honours by re-christening the owner. He was now referred to as Jacques le Merc.

His ownership of the vehicle had been a mistake, the result of an incorrect bid at the local auction, where Jacques had gone for a freezer cabinet to supplement the unit at his shop. Surprised a having made a successful bid, he hastened to pay the auctioneer and, having passed his bidding ticket through the sliding window of the office, he was given a receipt. He then drove his open truck to the compound to collect his freezer unit and handed his receipt to the clerk.

The clerk, a local man, was fully aware of Jacques's requirement; Jacques was his local shopkeeper and they had talked about it in the shop for days. He was more than a little surprised when he compared the ticket number with the freezer number and found they didn't tally. He remembered that this had happened once before when there had been two units of the same item. His surprise turned to amazement, when, comparing the ticket number against the auction list, he found that his shopkeeper friend had not only lost the bid for the freezer unit, but had purchased a beautiful Mercedes motorcar.

"Of course a mistake has been made," Jacques said to the clerk. "It just means exchanging the labels."

"Exchanging the labels!" The clerk exclaimed. "But Jacques, the freezer unit has already been collected and here is the ticket." He showed Jacques an unfamiliar number.

"You will have to get it back then," insisted Jacques, starting to lose his patience.

Tired of arguing the clerk brought the auctioneer.

"Monsieur, we shall soon be closing the compound and any articles remaining will be taken to the scrap heap," the Auctioneer said. "I have nothing further to say."

Reluctantly Jacques had gone to look at his purchase. He couldn't believe his eyes. He just stood in amazement, absorbed by what he considered to be the most beautiful motorcar in existence.

Hearing that the gates of the compound were being locked, he was forced to accustom himself to the luxury seating and slowly drive his possession home.

The joy of ownership, however, was not to continue unabated. Sadly, he found that for every ten litres of fuel he fed into the fuel tank, he could only travel ten kilometres. This severely restricted his plans for prestigious journeys to the city and back; instead he had to be content with intermittent trips to the local shops.

Jacques lived in a small mining village set among the vineyards of Burgundy, just four kilometres from the main autoroute leading to the Mediterranean. It was in this direction that he was currently travelling, to purchase his weekly fuel allocation.

The petrol station was situated just off the freeway and attracted only those seeking to save a dollar or two on their fuel costs and who were, in addition, prepared to queue on the restricted forecourt. It wasn't a satisfactory situation for Jacques, as, whilst he exercised considerable care in ensuring he arrived at the quietest part of the day, his car needed the space of two pumping islands in order to access the tank with ease. Today, a German transcontinental coach was occupying one of the islands.

The driver of the coach, having observed Jacques's arrival, was absorbed by the sheer beauty of the Mercedes. Walking over to the vehicle he stood carefully inspecting the bodywork, gently tapping it as if to check the thickness of metal. He then turned to the wheels, examining the chrome plating. Finally he took a close look at the translucent windows before standing back and viewing the complete vehicle from some distance away.

"Excusez-moi, Monsieur, can I help?" shouted Jacques, lowering the driver's window.

Ignoring Jacques's question, the driver returned to his coach, which by now had been removed from the pump area and was parked at the side of Jacques's car. Donning a suit of overalls the driver then stretched out full length on the forecourt and closely examined every centimetre of the front and rear bumpers of the Mercedes. He then made his way along the chassis sides and the wheel arches.

By this time Jacques had given up his quest for petrol, and again directed his remarks to the driver. "Pardon Monsieur. Is there something wrong?" he asked in a firm and positive voice that demanded a response.

The driver immediately turned to Jacques and speaking in a deep Bavarian voice, "Guten tag mein herr, my apologies, but is this your motor vehicle?"

"Ah. Oui," said Jacques. "Why do you enquire?"

Ignoring Jacques's direct question the driver reached into his pocket and took out a large wad of Euro dollars. He counted off Euro 5,000, took hold of Jacques's hand, placed the notes in it and firmly closed his fingers.'

"My friend," he said, looking Jacques straight in the eyes. "Promise me, that one week from today, you will return to this very spot with this motor car. You must promise."

Jacques was thunderstruck. He opened his fingers to make sure that he had seen aright, and the driver again took hold of Jacques's hand, and closed his fingers on the money.

"That is for you, in good faith that you will return with your vehicle in one week's time," he said. Then, turning, he climbed into his cab, and drove away.

By evening, Jacques's meeting with the coach driver was the talk of the village. There had been an accident involving Jacques the Merc, the silly old fool, some said. Others guessed that some idiot had made him an offer for his car. There were even those who said that he had turned down the offer.

Jacques was in a pensive mood. What a strange thing to happen, he thought. He hadn't as yet made up his mind whether next week should be an occasion to be embraced or not.

"I was given EU 5,000, by a driver at the petrol station today," he told his wife.

"Pardon mon cheri?" was the response.

"EU dollars, 5,000," replied Jacques.

"Whatever for?" was the immediate reply from his wife.

"I have to deliver the car to the petrol station again next week at the same time. He is probably bringing someone to see it." Jacques could only guess, he didn't really know what to expect.

Being the businesswoman of the family, Jacques's wife was a little suspicious, "Mon cher, have you had a valuation elsewhere?" she asked. "You can't be too careful."

"Perhaps I should," Jacques retorted. "I'll take a look around during the week."

That night his wife, Janette, was first to bed, allowing Jacques to give more thought to the conversation he had had with the coach driver.

It was 2 am before he retired. He then fell into a deep, satisfying sleep and was unaware of the intruder lifting the latch on his unlocked garage doors.

The man was young and agile and, in accordance with his cabled instructions from Italy, he slipped noiselessly into the garage and carried out the exact same examination that had been done previously, by the driver of the continental coach. Then, his examination complete, the intruder noiselessly dropped the latch on the garage door, and left.

As the days went by the strange happenings at the petrol station started to haunt Jacques. Was his car safe? Why had the driver parted with his money so readily?

Even his wife could see the anxious look that was developing on her husband's face.

"My love, why don't you take the car to your friend in Lyons?" she suggested. "He is a professional engineer and you will feel more confident of its condition once you have had it approved."

" I don't think anything less would satisfy me," Jacques agreed. "Shall we take a shopping trip? It may be a long job."

"If it would satisfy you, my love. I do have many things to do here, but yes, let's go." She too needed that assurance that all was well with her husband's plaything.

'Sheet Metal Workers and Engineers' the sign said, and after a pleasing reception from Jacques's friend, they were told they need not wait. They could return home and the car would be delivered back to them later in the day, or early the following day. As a deposit to cover the cost of their work Jacques gave them an endorsed cheque for EU5,000.True to his word his friend had the car delivered early the following morning with a full and detailed report of his findings and the EU.5,000 deposit returned in its entirety.

Jacques could now relax. He could continue his hitherto short journeys with full confidence. In fact the car felt easier to drive, lighter on the wheel. Janette had certainly been right to suggest that the professionals take a look, thought Jacques.

Life returned to normal and Jacques nearly forgot his promise to the driver of the Trans Continental coach. But, on the day previous to his appointment, he and his wife were enjoying a leisurely meal and a bottle of their favourite wine when they heard a commotion at the front of their house.

"You have visitors, my love. I will remove our meal until later." In a flash the table was cleared.

"Jacques Le Pretre?" came the question after a polite knock on the door.

"Yes," answered Jacques, "that is so." He detected a slight Italian accent, but what really impressed him was the air of opulence that surrounded his two visitors. He had never seen such immaculately dressed men. They were not only well dressed but had the correct accessories to match their formal attire. The diamond solitaire rings that decorated their fingers were by far the largest he had ever seen, and the gold Rolex watches and tiepins attracted similar attention.

"May we come in?" asked the elder of the two. Jacques placed them both midway between their fiftieth and sixtieth birthdays.

"I am sorry, yes, please come in. Would you care for a glass of wine?"

"No. It is kind of you to offer but we are in a hurry. I understand you are the proud owner of this Mercedes?" he said showing a picture of Jacques's car.

Jacques spent an eventful half hour with his visitors.

When they finally returned to their meal, Janette looked questioningly at her husband. "Well, aren't you going to tell me what happened? Who were they? Where had they come from?"

A broad grin appeared across her husband's face. "They bought the car," he answered.

"They what?" she asked.

"The car. They gave me Euro $5,000 for it."

"Mon Dieu! But why?"

"They wouldn't say. They collected the car and left. They also threw in a brand new Mercedes."

She couldn't believe this. But the statement was proved by the simple act of pulling back the curtains. She was confronted with a glistening grey Mercedes. She sighed, "Life will never be the same again, my love," she said, kissing her husband on his shiny bald patch.

Saturday came in due course and Jacques honoured his promise to the driver of the Trans Continental coach and proudly presented his new motorcar, telling the story of the sale that had been accomplished.

"Yes, I know what happened," said the coach driver. "But, my friend, did you recognise the man who paid you a visit?"

Shaking his head, "No," Jacques answered, feeling a little anxious. Taking a newspaper from his pocket the driver opened it out in full on the bonnet of the Mercedes and pointed to the full-length picture of Jacques's visitor. He was the head of the Italian Mafia and had been searching for this car for years.

The driver closed the newspaper smiling, and whispered into Jacques ear, "It was reported at the time that the car held the proceeds of a big bank job that had gone wrong. Five million dollars in gold, they said."

"That so?" said Jacques in cautious response.

The driver walked towards his coach, his head bowed in deep contemplation.

Jacques turned and opened the door of his car and took his seat at the driver's wheel. He looked into the mirror and saw on his face a smile, which had hitherto been a rare visitor to his wrinkled countenance.

He sat there for a moment or two longer, then, letting in the clutch, he cast a glance at the brand new gold Rolex watch, gracing his left wrist and the new diamond in in his tie. "So much my friend?" He murmured to himself. "So much?"

The End

108